W9-CKW-584

LOVE FROM UNCLE CLYDE

LOVE FROM UNCLE CLYDE

story and pictures by

Nancy Winslow Parker

DODD, MEAD & COMPANY
New York

Library of Congress Cataloging in Publication Data

Parker, Nancy Winslow.
    Love from Uncle Clyde.

    SUMMARY: A little boy receives a hippopotamus
from his Uncle Clyde in Africa for his birthday with
instructions on how to take care of it.
    [1. Hippopotamus—Fiction]   I. Title.
PZ7.P2274Lo   [E]   76-54957
ISBN 0-396-07426-X

for Becky, Barry, Judy Bea,
Charlie, Steve, and Virginia

LOVE FROM UNCLE CLYDE

Happy Birthday to Charlie
from Uncle Clyde.

I know you are going to love Elfreda.

She should have a drink of water as soon as she is unpacked. Enclosed is an envelope of Zambezi River snails for flavor.

You will find she likes a daily walk.

She loves children

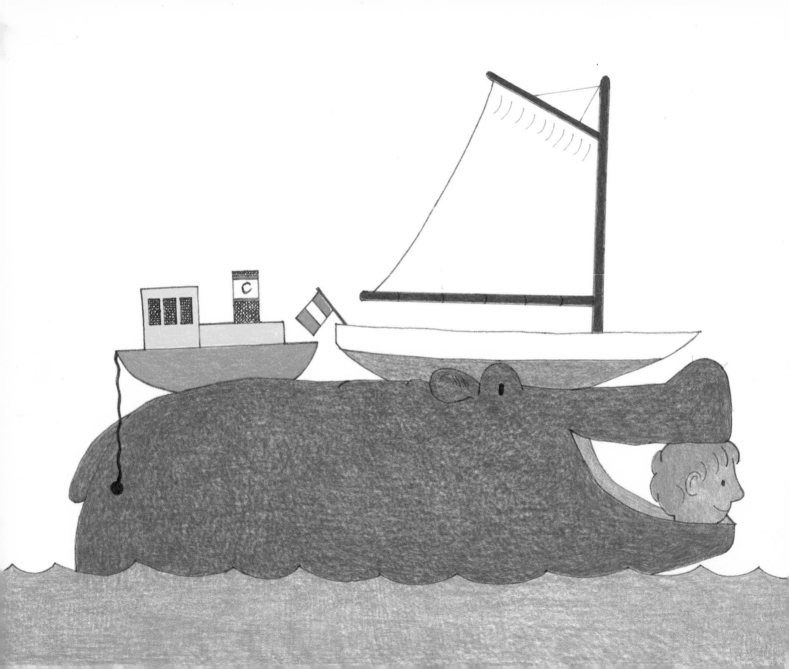

and the water.

Feed her three times a day.

Wash her often to keep her skin moist

and teeth free from tartar.

Show her every consideration you would if
she were your baby sister or brother,

and she will reward you with hours of
enjoyment.

Love from Uncle Clyde.

Written and illustrated by Nancy Winslow Parker

THE MAN WITH THE TAKE-APART HEAD

THE PARTY AT THE OLD FARM

MRS. WILSON WANDERS OFF

Illustrated by Nancy Winslow Parker

OH, A-HUNTING WE WILL GO
by John Langstaff

WARM AS WOOL, COOL AS COTTON
by Carter Houck

THE GOAT IN THE RUG
by Charles L. Blood and Martin Link

WILLY BEAR
by Mildred Kantrowitz

SWEETLY SINGS THE DONKEY
Selections by John Langstaff

THE SUBSTITUTE
by Ann Lawler